Woe is Moe

by **Diane Stanley**
illustrated by **Elise Primavera**

G. P. Putnam's Sons

To Amy Lemen
my nifty niece —D. S.

Moe worked at the Frozen Cow ice cream factory. So did his best friend, Arlene. They hated it there. Frozen Cow was probably the worst ice cream ever made. Even the artificial ingredients weren't real.

The only good part was that Moe and Arlene could work together. And every Friday they would celebrate the end of the week at Mr. Chang's Happy-All Chinese restaurant.

They always sat at the same table. And they always ordered the same things: wonton soup, steamed dumplings, and cold noodles with Hunan sauce.

One Friday, Moe asked Arlene if she had entered the slogan contest at the factory.

"No," Arlene said. "I heard a rumor that the prize was a gallon of Frozen Cow ice cream."

"Gosh, I hope not," said Moe. "I was hoping I'd win." He opened his fortune cookie. "Hey, listen to this! 'GREAT CHANGES WILL TAKE PLACE IN YOUR LIFE.' What do you suppose will happen?"

"Whatever it is," said Arlene, "it's bound to be good—isn't it?"

After dinner, as usual, they went to the Roxy to take in a movie.

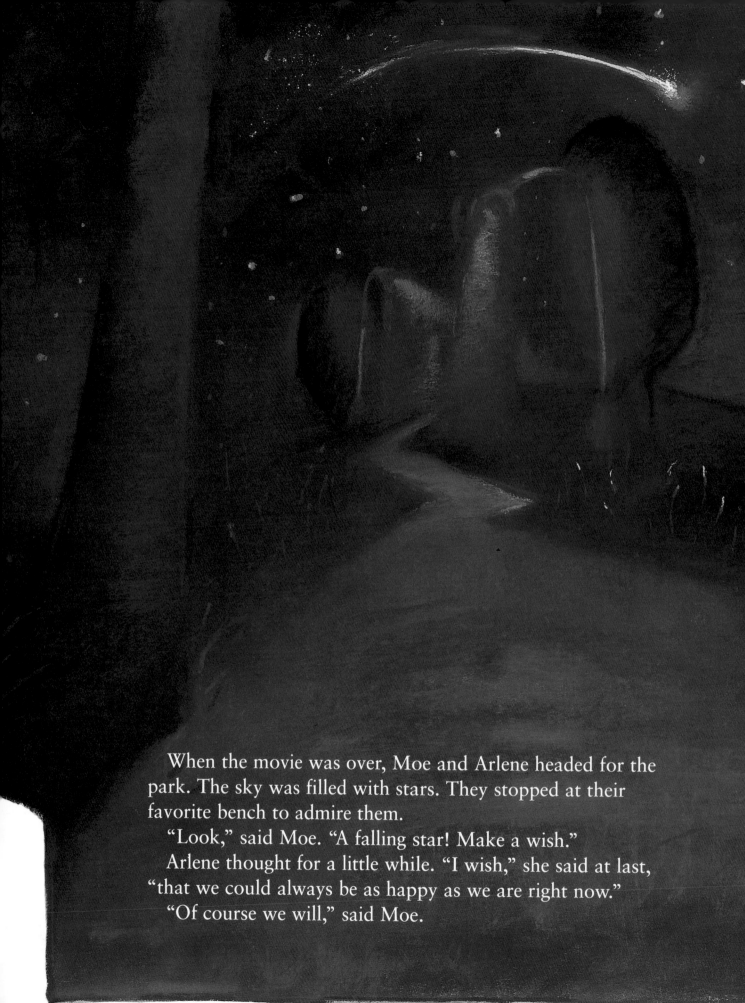

When the movie was over, Moe and Arlene headed for the
park. The sky was filled with stars. They stopped at their
favorite bench to admire them.

"Look," said Moe. "A falling star! Make a wish."

Arlene thought for a little while. "I wish," she said at last,
"that we could always be as happy as we are right now."

"Of course we will," said Moe.

On Monday, Moe hurried to work. That was the day he would find out if he had won the contest.

At about ten o'clock Moe was called to the boss's office.

He didn't come back. Arlene was worried.

At last the whistle blew, and everyone could go home. Arlene grabbed her purse and her lunch box and ran for the door.

Moe was there waiting for her. She was so glad to see him she gave him a big hug.

"What happened?" she cried.

"I won the contest!" he said proudly. "I can't talk now, but I have big news. I'll tell you all about it tonight." And he hurried off.

Moe had reserved the best table at a fancy restaurant. Arlene felt underdressed.

After they had ordered, Moe told her what had happened. "I have a new job! The boss thought my slogan was so original that he decided to make me vice-president in charge of advertising. Just think of it—I'll be rich! I'll have a limousine and a big office! Important people will want to know me!"

"Gosh," said Arlene, softly.

Arlene didn't see Moe all week. She missed him.

Finally he called. There was a lot of static on the line.

"Moe, where are you calling from?"

"My car phone," he said. "Hold on, we're heading into a tunnel. . . . Arlene? Are you still there? Sorry about that. Hey, guess what? I'm moving uptown. I've got a penthouse with a river view."

"Great, Moe!" Arlene shouted over the static.

"Wait till you see all my new stuff!"

"Great, Moe."

"Hey, gotta go. Catch you later!" He hung up.

"Great, Moe . . ." Arlene whispered.

Months passed and Arlene didn't hear a word from Moe. When her birthday rolled around, she called to invite him to her party.

"This is Moe," said the voice on the other end of the line.

"Hi, Moe!" said Arlene. But Moe went right on talking.

"I'm away on important business, so I can't take your call right now. If you're calling about the 'Just say *yes* to Frozen Cow' campaign, press 'one' *now*. If you're calling to request an interview, press 'two' *now*. If you wish to speak to an operator..."

Arlene hung up and had a good cry.

Moe was in Paris trying to sell Frozen Cow to the French. This was difficult, because if there is one thing the French care about, it's food. They know bad ice cream when they taste it.

Moe went to lots of parties. He started wearing sunglasses, even at night, because that was what the cool people did. Unfortunately, the glasses made it hard for him to see, and he fell into fountains from time to time.

The people he met were rich and beautiful. They were also bored and miserable. Moe fit right in. He was relieved when Frozen Cow gave up on the French and let him go home.

When he got back to his penthouse, Moe found a Happy-All takeout menu, which had been slipped under the door. Moe sat down in his designer chair and looked at his river view. He felt very, very lonely and very, very tired. He picked up the phone and dialed.

"I'd like an order of wonton soup, some steamed dumplings, and cold noodles with Hunan sauce," Moe said.

"Is this Moe?" asked Mr. Chang.

"Yes. Yes, it is," said Moe.

"You sound terrible," said Mr. Chang.

"I feel terrible," said Moe. "Long hours. Smoke-filled rooms. Jet lag. Loneliness..."

"Stay right where you are," said Mr. Chang. "My new chef has just what you need!"

After a while Moe's doorbell rang.

"Chicken soup," said the delivery person, "Chinese style!"

Moe ate the soup gratefully. It made him feel better. The dumplings and the noodles were just as he remembered them. While he drank his tea, he opened his fortune cookie. It read: FOR THE ANSWER TO YOUR PROBLEMS, FIND OUT WHAT'S PLAYING AT THE MOVIES.

"How mysterious!" thought Moe. He headed for the Roxy.

When he got to the theater, the woman behind the ticket counter called him over. "You must be Moe," she said. "I have a package for you." It was a little bag, and inside was another fortune cookie.

TO BE HAPPY, GO TO YOUR FAVORITE BENCH IN THE PARK, it said.

Moe certainly had a favorite bench, so off he went.

It was a lovely, cool night. Moe looked up and saw that the sky was filled with stars. They made him think of Arlene. He missed her very much.

When he got to their special bench, he found a paper bag sitting on it.

"More and more mysterious," he thought. It held yet another fortune cookie!

Where you find the best noodles you will also find happiness.

That could be only one place. Moe hurried to Happy-All. Mr. Chang met him at the door.

"Moe," he said, "long time no see! Come in and meet my new chef. She bakes the best fortune cookies in town." He led Moe over to his old table. There sat Arlene.

Moe's jaw dropped. "So it was *you*!" he said.

"Yes, Moe, it was me. And I baked you one last cookie. Here—read it."

Moe broke it open and took out the little slip of paper. "'I WILL ALWAYS BE YOUR BEST FRIEND,'" he read.

Arlene smiled. "I'll always be your best friend, too," she said, and gave Moe a great big hug.

Text copyright © 1995 by Diane Stanley. Illustrations copyright © 1995 by Elise Primavera
All rights reserved. This book, or parts thereof, may not be reproduced in any form without permission in writing
from the publisher. G. P. Putnam's Sons, a division of The Putnam & Grosset Group, 200 Madison Avenue,
New York, NY 10016. G. P. Putnam's Sons, Reg. U.S. Pat. & Tm. Off. Published simultaneously in Canada.
Printed in Hong Kong by South China Printing Co. (1988) Ltd. Text set in Sabon Roman.
Library of Congress Cataloging-in-Publication Data. Stanley, Diane. Woe is Moe / written by Diane Stanley; illustrated by Elise Primavera.   p.   cm.
Summary: Moe's new job in advertising at the ice cream factory brings him money, travel, and prestige—so why is he lonely and miserable?
[1. Dogs—Fiction. 2. Friendship—Fiction. 3. Success—Fiction.] I. Primavera, Elise, ill. II. Title.   PZ7.S7869Wo 1995   [E]—dc20 94-3765 CIP AC
ISBN 0-399-22699-0
1   3   5   7   9   10   8   6   4   2
First Impression